Arm in arm, bride and groom headed down the aisle, striding to the martial strains of the wedding march. . . .

The candles all through the sanctuary abruptly flared to life. Their flames leapt up six feet into the air. The congregation cowered away from this new assault, and the trumpets and drums faltered into silence. In the agonized dying of the bagpipes came human shrieks—

Fiery figures formed in the flaring candles: warriors, dressed in armor, their swords drawn.

FORGOTTEN REALMS®

Fantasy Adventure

THE DOUBLE DIAMOND TRIANGLE SAGA™

Fantasy Adventure

THE DOUBLE DIAMOND TRIANGLE SAGA™

Part 1

THE
ABDUCTION

J. Robert King

THE ABDUCTION
©1998 TSR, Inc.
All Rights Reserved.

Distributed to the book trade in the United States by Random House, Inc. and in Canada by Random House of Canada Ltd. Distributed to the hobby, toy, and comic trade in the United States and Canada by regional distributors. Distributed worldwide by Wizards of the Coast, Inc. and regional distributors.

Cover art by Heather LeMay.

FORGOTTEN REALMS and the TSR logo are registered trademarks owned by TSR, Inc. DOUBLE DIAMOND TRIANGLE SAGA is a trademark owned by TSR, Inc.

All TSR characters, character names, and the distinctive likenesses thereof are trademarks owned by TSR, Inc.

TSR, Inc. is a subsidiary of Wizards of the Coast, Inc.

First Printing: January 1998
Printed in the United States of America.
Library of Congress Catalog Card Number: 96-90564

9 8 7 6 5 4 3 2 1
8634XXX1501

ISBN: 0-7869-0864-5

U.S., CANADA, ASIA,
PACIFIC, & LATIN AMERICA
Wizards of the Coast, Inc.
P.O. Box 707
Renton, WA 98057-0707
+1-206-624-0933

EUROPEAN HEADQUARTERS
Wizards of the Coast, Belgium
P.B. 34
2300 Turnhout
Belgium
+32-14-44-30-44

Visit our website at **www.tsr.com**

For Ed Greenwood,
Lord Mage of the Realms

Prelude

Reflections

How has this happened?

In one evening, I have been transformed from Pier-geiron Paladinson, Open Lord of Waterdeep, into this . . . this inward-shrinking worm. Worse—my palace, my city, and my world have transformed around me.

My palace slumps into sand.

Waterdeep melts into air.

Toril sloughs away.

. . . I blame it on the dust. The will of dust has changed. The chorus of specks no longer sings, "I cling to thee." Every mote has turned traitor. Rock becomes sand. Sand becomes dust. Dust becomes nothing at all. The particles have denounced their kinship. What once bound all to all is gone. . . .

Oh, to sleep. . . .

I should have expected transformations. After all, I had chosen to orbit a changeable star.

Eidola. She is changeable in all things—mood and mind, will and wont. Only her beauty remains the same.

I comfort myself with the thought of her beauty.

Somewhere, her bright, silvery eyes look upon something. Somewhere, her long auburn hair casts its shadow on some rock or blade of grass. Her smile, with its thousand mysteries and thousand thousand promises, somewhere enchants someone.

I tell myself that somewhere, she breathes.

She must breathe. Her beauty is eternal. It is the same beauty that Shaleen had, the beauty that lives on in Eidola. . . .

No, I must not think that.

Eidola's beauty is her own.

Eidola's beauty is immortal.

She will not die like Shaleen.

Will not die, or *has not died?* What sorrows fill the transforming tense of words!

Oh, to sleep. . . .

I met Eidola in a dream.

I wore full plate armor. My white stallion, Dreadnought, was resplendently barded. Even the summer woods had put on their best: velvet mosses, pendulous cones, carpets of gold. . . . Insects whispered in the heavy afternoon.

A scream shattered the stillness. It was a high, helpless sound. Someone was cornered, crying out in mortal terror.

I halted Dreadnought. I listened. The woods were filled with ghost echoes. Then a damnable stillness settled.

Dreadnought huffed. His satiny back twitched.

A rustling came in the trailside trees. With it came another terrified scream.

A woman, I thought . . . a beautiful, helpless lady trapped in some old ruined tower . . . beset on all sides by blackguards . . . the stuff of dreams.

"Ho, Dreadnought," I called.

The great stallion was already galloping toward the sound.

When I saw the woman at the tree, I thought of Shaleen. Her hair was the auburn of an autumn evening. Her teeth had the gleam of pearls. She was armored in well-worn field plate.

And, like Shaleen, she was anything but helpless.

Ignoring me, the woman grabbed a tree in front of her and shook it. Another scream came from above.

I looked up, and saw a scaly kobold clinging there.

"You can't have your money back!" the puny creature shouted. It shook its lizardlike head and angrily jangled a coin purse.

I stepped down from Dreadnought. I walked toward the woman. "Unless that purse holds a fortune in gold, you'd best let him go, Shaleen."

She cast a silent reproof my way, and shook the tree again.

In apology, I took out my battle-axe and began chopping the trunk. It shuddered with each blow and started to lean. I wiped sweat from my face and chopped again. Only when the tree crackled and fell did I look up toward the kobold.

It was gone. While I had chopped, the woman had used a snip of jerky to coax the thief down. Now, woman and monster sat side by side like old friends, eating meat and watching me sweat.

I laughed and joined them.

She had lured a kobold and a man.

I became her willing captive.

Her name was Eidola. *Is* Eidola. *Is, is!* What sorrows fill the transforming tense of words!

She is gone. My benevolent captor is gone. My changeable star has fled, cometlike, or winked out altogether.

Perhaps her will has changed with the will of the dust, the fleeting and incomprehensible migration of minute attractions.

Oh, to sleep. . . .

Chapter 1

Perils in the Palace

Laskar Nesher, a fat nobleman with an illicit logging empire, led his family toward the gate to Piergeiron's palace. The brown waistcoat he wore was just snug enough to make him look like a bratwurst, and his jowls were red from chafing on his lapels. A slender consort clung to his side. She was half his age, one fifth his bulk, and twice as quick with coin. Behind them trudged a teenaged boy who oozed boredom and fashionable disaffection.

Laskar halted before the gate guard and presented his invitation:

Master and Friend Laskar Nesher, and Heir Kastonoph Nesher:
The honor of your presence is requested at the marriage of Piergeiron Paladinson, Open Lord of Waterdeep, and Eidola of Neverwinter, Descendent of Boarskyr. The wedding will take place the Seventeenth and Eighteenth Days of Eleint, this Year of the Haunting.
Please arrive by third watch on the Seventeenth, an hour before sunset. The feasting will begin at nightfall, the masked ball thereafter, as stomachs allow, and the nuptials at the stroke of midnight on the Eighteenth. Sandrew the Wise, Savant of Oghma at the Font of Knowledge, and Khelben "Blackstaff" Arunsun, High Mage of Waterdeep, will officiate.

"Have you brought any weapons?" the guard asked levelly.

Laskar said, "Of course not. We'd not bring—"

"I suppose I'd best surrender this," broke in the youth, handing over a sheathed dagger. "And while you're peace-stringing mine, you might as well do Father's, too."

Laskar flushed, even redder than before. He struggled at his belt for a moment and handed over his once-hidden blade.

The guard finished tying the youth's dagger into its sheath and did the same for the father's. "Anything else?"

Before Laskar could answer, a shadowy figure standing

in the gateway said, "No. Nor do they bear any harmful magics."

Startled, the Neshers turned. They had not noticed the black-robed and gray-bearded mage. The wizard gave a nod of approval to young Kastonoph.

The lad returned the nod, blood draining from his face. "Good evening, Lord Mage Arunsun," he managed to say.

"Good evening to you," replied the mage. "For your honesty, you, young Kastonoph, can call me Khelben, or, perhaps, Blackstaff."

The lad stood a moment longer, gaping in disbelief. His father quickly gathered him in and herded the youth past the hawkeyed wizard and through the open gates.

Beyond lay a hall, high and bright. Slender pillars ran in colonnades along its sides. An elegant fan vault arched overhead. Across the polished floor of marble, silken gowns slid beside worsted robes of state. In one corner of the room, citterns and gitterns and fifes serenaded the guests, who added their happy babble to the music. The place overflowed with the sounds of the best people conversing with their betters.

"Another dull noble wedding," groaned Kastonoph—or Noph as he was known to all but his father. His amazement was gone, replaced by a practiced mask of cynicism. "Common lads my age are out smiting dragons, making tragic deals with fiends, and rescuing their lady-loves from warlocks."

Laskar rarely listened to his discontented offspring. For decades, the man had heeded nothing but the jingle of coins. "Please don't make your presence at this affair

more scandalous than your absence would have been."
Laskar had coined this turn of phrase some five years
back. He liked it so well, he used it every chance he got.

Noph made a rude sign as he scratched his cheek.

His father's consort knew the boy at least as well as she
did the man. "Noph, why don't you take a look about?
There's no more dangerous company in Undermountain
than you'll find here in the palace tonight."

Noph blinked at her. Though he hated Stelar for
openly squandering his father's money—Noph's own in-
heritance—the woman was perceptive, shrewd, scan-
dalously fun, and at five years his elder, an honest beauty.
Noph knew she was trying to get rid of him, but he half-
expected she spoke the truth about the perils in Piergeiron's
palace.

Nodding knowingly to her, he made a quick exit.

The heir of the Nesher estate had just rounded one slim
column of the room when he heard his father's voice ask,
"Where's that brat off to now?"

Stelar's reply was appeasing. "Oh, off to save Faerûn
again, I'm sure."

* * * * *

The white-suited groom, Piergeiron Paladinson, and
his eight-foot-tall bodyguard, Madieron Sunderstone,
headed past banqueting tables filled with nobles and
guildmasters. Or, at least, they *tried* to head past. Every
one of the guests stopped Piergeiron to ask a favor.

The guests had been sitting long enough to become en-
trenched and fidgety. Forks, knives, and other weaponry

lay tantalizingly close. Roasted boar taunted from steaming platters. The very air smelled of opportunity—all of it just out of reach. This combination of heightened appetites and suppressed activities conspired to make the guests aggressive, suspicious, and covetous of Piergeiron's attentions. Until they could feast on boar, they would dine on groom.

First had been the Neshers—lumber money of the most vulgar kind. Piergeiron noted the conspicuous absence of their ever-prodigal son, Noph, the most pleasant member of an unpleasant crew. Laskar Nesher ended his greeting with a request to be moved closer to the elven nobles of the High Forest. He hoped to "trick the longears" into bartering away logging rights.

Ever the diplomat, Piergeiron answered with a tactful version of, "Not if Ao himself commanded it."

The elves, perhaps not out of longear-shot, insinuated that at Piergeiron's *next* wedding, he should avoid inviting tree killers and stone hackers.

To that, the Open Lord replied enigmatically that many current guests would be excluded, should there be a "next wedding."

As to the stone hackers—dwarves who considered themselves descended from Delzoun—they requested only prompter refills of their ale mugs. Already, they had drained a quarter barrel apiece!

Piergeiron sighed and ruefully rubbed his shock of black hair. There would be a few more tufts of gray in it after tonight. Surviving his own wedding, and making sure the rest of the celebrants did, would be his greatest feat of statesmanship yet.

"I will arrange for a tapped barrel to be placed on your table," he told the dwarves before continuing on.

Not all the annoyances were this harmless. After departing the dwarves and before encountering the next barrage, Piergeiron turned to his mop-headed bodyguard.

"Keep your eyes sharp."

That advice seemed ill-considered, given the sheepdog locks dangling in Madieron's eyes, but the bodyguard nodded dutifully.

Piergeiron continued. "I've gotten wind of plots against the trade pact. It must be sealed tonight. Some factions would cause any disturbance to prevent it. But, more than the pact, I fear for Eidola. Guarding me means keeping one eye on her."

Madieron's eyes struggled askew beneath his bangs. "Got it, milord," he said.

The Open Lord nodded dubiously. Madieron was a good man, as steady, strong, patient, and smart as a rock. Piergeiron was his close match in battle, but tonight he'd supply the more cerebral virtues for the pair. Between the two of them, they were ready for anything.

A tremendous clangor of silver tea services and overturned platters rang from the end of the banquet hall, along with a shriek that stilled the chatter and bustle of the party.

With none of their previous decorum, Piergeiron and his bodyguard shouldered past the guests, who were too busy gasping or rising to their feet to detain them. The room went deathly silent except for the scud of chairs, the clank of Madieron's war-shod feet, and the sound of angry voices—three male and one . . . one . . .

"Eidola," Piergeiron croaked out, rushing toward his bride.

His cry, hoarse though it was, settled all din for a moment. Piergeiron pushed past the wall of gawkers that had formed around the disturbance. Beyond was a strange tableau.

Eidola stood at her place setting, fury on her face. Her ire was directed at a little hooded fellow whose arms were pinned back by a pair of doorguards. The center of Eidola's magnificent gown was stained with tea—ruined satin amid wet pearls and lace.

In three rapid strides, Piergeiron had reached the cowled man and flung back his hood. The face that appeared had a koboldesque quality—wide-eyed, feckless, and scaled with acne—but it belonged to an all-too-human wizard.

"Forgive me," the adept pleaded piteously, tears running down his face. "I-I just wanted to help."

"Help?" raged one of the guards. "Look at the lady's dress. It is ruined!"

The lad had the smell of honesty about him—honesty in the form of sheer terror. Piergeiron laid a massive hand on his shoulder and rumbled, "Speak, lad—the truth. You'll be punished for whatever you've done here, but will be punished for more than that if you lie."

Blood drained from the young mage's cheeks. "Sire, she'd told her maidservant that the tea was cold. I cast a little spell to warm it—"

"Spells are forbidden, as are loose weapons," Piergeiron said. "That alone is grave offense."

"I know, I know," cried the lad miserably. "But I only

wanted to help. The maidservant was so frightened by my hand gestures, she dumped the platter, all over—" his trembling hand indicated where the tea had landed.

Piergeiron scowled. This lad was either an accomplished actor or a novice adept. "Where is the maidservant?"

The mage glanced from side to side, at a loss. "She was here a moment ago. I could have sworn—"

With an impulsive whirl of her tea-stained petticoats, Eidola spun and hurried off to her chambers.

"Guards, take this man to the dungeons for questioning," Piergeiron said. He turned to his ever-present bodyguard. "Madieron, you go with them. I'm off on private business."

The man-mountain nodded his haystack of hair and followed the guards.

Meanwhile Piergeiron turned and stalked after Eidola, his heart rumbling strangely. "I'm right behind you!" he called to his bride. He passed into the vestibule beyond, Eidola's skirts rustling ahead of him.

Before him and beyond Eidola, he spied the fearful face of a serving girl. The lass gasped and bolted down the hall. Eidola snatched up a torch from its sconce and ran after her.

Neither woman spared a glance back. The maid fled around a corner. Eidola followed in a whisper of white lace. Piergeiron could not keep up. He rounded the corner. A dead-end hall lay beyond, and in it, Eidola, facing down the maid.

The girl held her hands out before her as though in apology, but her fingernails were flexed, clawlike.

"Forgive me. It's just a little tea," the servant mewled. "I got so scared when I spilt it—"

"What is your name?" demanded Piergeiron, stepping slowly forward. "Who hired you? When did you start? *What is your name?*"

Eidola did not even await a reply, lunging with the fiery brand.

The torch arced toward upraised hands that became talons, with claws as long as scythe blades. Those claws caught the burning brand and held it. The maid's smooth throat transformed into a long, plate-covered thing with hard shells and thick black hairs sprouting from it. The woman's young face changed into the hoary-jowled head of a greater jackal. Her livery split to reveal a canine body.

"A shapeshifter!" cried Piergeiron. He drew his ornamental long sword, Halcyon, snapping the peace-strings with a mighty yank, and dived between the beast and his bride.

The gnoll-creature raked Piergeiron with its brutal claws. Razor-tipped nails shrieked across silver armor and sent showers of sparks to the floor. A talon snagged on his armor and tore free.

The creature began a howl of rage. Piergeiron thrust with Halcyon. The beast spun away. A jab that would have split its heart lanced its side instead.

The thing began to transform again. Its shaggy feet became cloven hooves, its legs the haunches of a goat, its belly bald and red. . . .

Though the transformation swept over the creature in a flash, Piergeiron struck again before the change was complete. His sword whirled through changing flesh and sliced into the monster's dark heart. Blood as black as ink shot forward, and the beast, in midtransformation, crumpled.

As it fell, Piergeiron drew forth his ornamental long sword. The blood in the filigreed etchings hissed like acid. Beyond the smoking blade, the monster lay still upon the floor.

Piergeiron knelt beside the thing, his sword yet at the ready as he checked it for breath.

"It's dead," he announced solemnly.

Piergeiron's bodyguard loped up behind Eidola and skidded to a halt. He puffed aside his jagged bangs and stared at the bride and groom, their hair wild and their faces streaming sweat. Then he glanced at the slain beast before them. Madieron turned as white as an albino rabbit.

Up behind him came two more guards, startled and breathless. "What is it?" gasped one.

"Malaugrym, or so I guess," said Piergeiron. "The Ones Who Watch. Shapeshifters from beyond Faerûn. They think this world their chessboard. They've brought down many rulers with ruses less devious than—" He suddenly stopped in choked realization. He turned toward his bride and embraced her. "You're safe. That . . . that thing must have been stalking you when the apprentice startled it. It must have thought he was casting a spell on it, perhaps stripping away the disguise."

Eidola lowered her torch so that it shed light on her dress. She stared ruefully at the stain.

"Guard this body," Piergeiron said to Madieron. "You two, find the Blackstaff and Sandrew the Wise. They'll want to check it over." He took his bride by the arm and gestured down the hall. "Shall we?"

Eidola nodded, and together the pair strolled away, as though walking from a sunny picnic in a park.

The two older guards turned knowing glances on the bodyguard. "It's a shame, you guarding this dead thing when you should be guarding the Open Lord."

Madieron flushed beneath his haystack of hair. He managed a half-shrug. "My orders." The corpse seemed to be slowly changing shape, shrinking and turning gray.

A friendly hand clapped onto Madieron's side. "Tell you what. I'll go get the Blackstaff and Sandrew, Harl here will guard the corpse, and you can get back to duty. The Open Lord shouldn't be unprotected, what with monsters like this roaming the palace."

Ever concerned about Piergeiron's safety, Madieron blinked in obvious relief, shrugged again, and rushed away after Piergeiron.

Smiling sarcastically, one of the guards waved the lumbering warrior away. By the time he disappeared around the corner, the waving hand had become a claw. . . .

Chapter 2
Masquerades

Noph saw it all.

He saw the maidservant flinch as the young wizard cast a spell, saw Eidola and Piergeiron follow the shapeshifter and battle it, saw the two guards form their hands into claws and drag the body to the nearest jakes.

And there was more, much more.

Peering past the half-closed door, Noph saw the guards fully transform into crablike things. Their eyes rose on

stalks above their horny skulls and their bodies became
hard and bristly. With their pinchers, they quickly shredded the body. They ate what they could—muscle and
gristle and brain. The rest, they fed down the jakes, into
the infamous sewers of Waterdeep. Noph imagined he
could hear the masticating jaws of even nastier things
below.

That was when he climbed up into the rafters.

Now, the monsters transformed again, into two different-
looking guards. The men effetely dabbed the last spots of
sizzling blood from their uniforms. In smug satisfaction,
they nodded to each other and walked back toward the
party, strolling beneath the spot where Noph crouched.

This noble wedding wasn't so boring after all.

Noph waited until the beasts were long gone before he
tried to get down. Though he tried to imitate the silent
grace of a cat, one leg cuff caught on a nail, and he did a
complete flip before crashing to the floor. He was on his
feet again before he knew if he could stand, and looked
quickly up and down the hall. The shapeshifting guards
were nowhere to be seen, and no one else was about. He
stood straight and brushed himself off, well pleased
despite the fall.

The sting of pride had quickly given place to the tingle
of anticipation. Mystery! Adventure! Paladins and
princesses and clawed villains!

He'd been lucky so far, happening upon the culprits in
the midst of their crimes. Now, though, the trail had gone
cold. Where should he go next to unravel this mystery?

Follow the money. That's what his father had always
advised. For Laskar Nesher, the money had led to disrep-

utable lumber deals. For shapeshifters, the money would lead to . . . the city treasury? No, someone wanting to get to the treasury would have posed as a guard, not as a maidservant. The only reason to masquerade as a maidservant was to get close to Eidola.

Yes, Eidola, but why?

Some Waterdhavians thought her a bad match for Piergeiron. Some even felt the Open Lord should be removed from office due to his lack of judgment. After all, the bedchamber is more persuasive than the council chamber. By marrying Piergeiron, this mystery woman could wield untold power over the city.

There were whispers of a price laid on her head.

That's it! Assassins! They'd infiltrated the ranks of the servants and the guards!

No, Noph thought a moment later. As appealing as it was to think of noble assassins, a shot from afar could kill more easily and safely than a monster disguised as a chambermaid. Besides, as guards and servants, the shapechanging creatures have had many other opportunities to kill Eidola and haven't done so.

They must want something else, Noph thought, and must need to get close to Eidola to get it. . . . But why?

Follow the money, Noph repeated to himself.

The much-touted trade route to Kara-Tur—now there was some money to be followed. Noph's father had said that final approval of the route depended on Eidola. The last holdouts against the pact were kin of Eidola, and they would sign only after she had married the Open Lord. If the marriage were prevented, the pact would not be complete. Then, the nobles and guilds would retain the economic dynasties they had worked so hard to build. That's where the money led, to the nobles and guilds.

"Ah, Father," Noph said to himself, "I'd not expected to find your kind among the monsters tonight."

Dusting off his hands, Noph set off for the banquet hall. At long last, he was interested in talking with his father's friends.

When he arrived in the feast hall, he approached a band of guildmasters who stood in the middle of the bustle, arrogantly smoking Maztican cigars and politely calling each other fools. The half-drunk merchants seemed engaged in a contest to see who could be the most boisterous, obstreperous, and opinionated. They made easy targets for an amateur eavesdropper.

". . . whole thing feels rushed, that's all. A mystery woman from Nowhere—"

"Not *Nowhere,* but *Neverwinter.*"

"—Just as I said, from Nowhere, and a hasty wedding and a hasty trade pact all rolled together—"

"That explains the haste: the Open Lord and Miss Mystery must have rolled together."

"—in which case all you can expect is a quick ceremony meant to cover for whatever bastards come crawling out of the woodwork, and by bastards I mean those damned Kara-Turian dragon-lovers—"

Noph moved away from that cluster. The man holding court there was a drunken braggart, who greedily gulped down misinformation and vomited it back as vintage lies. There was no treason in his empty bluster, but also no truth.

To one side of the hall, standing aloof from the gossiping horde, Noph saw a circle of paladins, clad in glittering silver chain mail. In awe he recognized among them Kern, a mighty warrior despite his youth, and Miltiades, once un-dead but now again among the living. Noph formally saluted the group and passed on.

Noph approached another group. He drifted nearby and turned about as if admiring some particular beauty. This conversation had a very different tenor:

"—not at all like it was. What is the point of overland trade? The oceans have been charted to Kara-Tur and beyond. We've felled enough forests to give us a matchless fleet and now we don't want to use any of the ships? I don't understand."

"Think how we feel, Mate. You're a landlubber—sure it's your money that sets sails on our rigs and get us where we go, but if you're out coin, think what you're out. Out a living, that's what. Used to be that seamen had a hard life, sure, but now, no life at all."

"Yes, which is why I thought, why wait? Why wait for a politician to pave the way—no pun intended. We've got all we need, just not official sanction. I thought, perhaps, to make five of our merchant ships into warships, send them down to grab the right bits of land—the capes and so forth—capture them, put up outposts, and there you have a water trade route. . . ."

Noph drifted away. These people were planning business, not treason. Certainly, it might be a fine line between the two, but Noph doubted these men were in league with regicidal traitors.

"—during the ball. . . . The crossbow is already in place. . . . I've said too much already. . . . No, we shouldn't be seen speaking . . . wait until we're masked—"

Noph paused, pretending to check the sole of his boot for something stuck to it. He listened a bit more.

The speaker was a woman, standing in the shadow behind a large, potted palm. Her voice had a strange burr that Noph had never heard before—something vaguely Calashite. He could see little of her appearance—only that she was of extraordinary height, with lean shoulders and a graceful figure.

Abruptly, she moved away from the palm, toward the great dance hall where the ball would be held. Noph watched the sway of her red dress for a moment before remembering to put his boot down and follow.

* * * * *

By the time Piergeiron had returned to the celebration—after discovering the disappearance of the shapeshifter's body—dinner was finished and the dancing had begun.

It was a masquerade.

Eidola herself had planned the masked ball, saying she wanted to dance with the groom without courting bad luck by seeing him before the ceremony.

The costumes were designed to provide complete anonymity. At the entrance to the ballroom, a curtain had been strung to make a dressing area between curtain and doors. One by one, the guests entered the changing area, donned loose gray robes over their clothes, and were fitted with full-head masks. The masks were grotesque— hawks, toads, dragons, bugbears, dwarves, elves, humans, gnomes—and they took their forms from all the creatures of Faerun.

By wearing these masks, the guests were, Eidola said, transformed into every manner of creature in the world. They became emissaries from Faerûn to the wedding couple, gathered to bless a marriage that would bring peace and prosperity to all creatures.

Such were the bride's lofty justifications of this masquerade. In truth, as each guest pushed back the double doors and joined the flocks of other grotesque beasts in the ballroom, the masks did not create a peaceable kingdom so much as an exotic jungle.

Piergeiron and Madieron stood in the dark dressing space outside the ballroom. All around them were small stands holding the heads of mammoths and pixies, treants and tigers. Their ghoulish grins made the Open Lord shiver.

Piergeiron was a straightforward man, and he didn't go much for elaborate charades. On the other hand, he had had no hope of prevailing over Eidola when it came to wedding arrangements.

Out of a dark corner of the dressing space, a bald-headed attendant slid toward Piergeiron. He pulled a gray robe over the groom's shoulders and the hilt of his sword. Piergeiron bristled. With assassins about, it was folly to let his sword get so fouled.

To add insult to injury, the costumer next appeared with an especially repellent mask for him to wear.

"A rat?" Piergeiron asked regretfully.

The clothier's bulbous head nodded eagerly on his skinny neck. "A Waterdhavian Sewer Rat. They are tenacious creatures. Brave. Almost noble . . . in their way."

Piergeiron stared at the glassy black eyes of the mask, the boars' teeth set in its maw, the mossy felt and pantomimed garbage dangling between those teeth. . . . "Isn't there something more suitable?"

The clothier reached up to set the mask in place. "The point of a masquerade is to be what you are not."

Piergeiron stoically suffered the placement of the rodent head over his own. When it was situated, he hesitantly asked, "How do I look?"

"Perfectly ratty," the man replied. "And what do you think of Madieron?"

Piergeiron looked up at his eight-foot-tall bodyguard and saw the fey smirk of a pixie.

The Open Lord broke into laughter. Madieron, unamused, unceremoniously thrust the man toward the double doors.

The Open Lord stumbled through the doors. The ballroom beyond gleamed with crystal chandeliers and moldings of gold. Masked dancers swirled across the floor in a two-step pavane. The ensemble of rebecs and fifes played a familiar dance cadence, though the tones they produced were twisted in the new Sembian fashion. Measured harmonies continually devolved into chaotic dissonances.

Still trying to catch his balance, Piergeiron took two full strides before stopping dead within the sweeping arm of the pavane. He felt as if he had stumbled onto a clockwork carousel. There he stood, frozen amidst radiant motion. The procession of creatures was dazzling— beholders, wraiths, lions, lizard men, griffons, owls, horses, camels, basilisks. . . . Staring at their shifting multitude, whirling in the dance, Piergeiron grew dizzy.

He dropped to one knee, struggling to see something familiar. Wasn't this his palace? It felt as though he had stumbled through a portal to some deviant jungle. Or perhaps, a madman's mind.

Hadn't Eidola planned this all?

His eyes found no relief. The pillars that lined the hall glowed with an ill green light that made them look like the ancient boles of green-sapped trees. Their acanthus-leaf tops and the riot of carved plaster across the ceiling became a dense canopy of foliage. The candles of the chandeliers glowed in pendulous bunches of exotic fruit. They sent up crazings of smoke, soot in place of pollen. Piergeiron wondered where these deadly spores would take root.

The touch of a hand—a feminine hand—drew the Open Lord from his crouch and set him into motion among the others.

Despite his dizziness, Piergeiron's feet fell into the duple rhythm of the pavane. He held the hand of the woman, an eel-headed thing, and swayed toward her and away from her.

"So, handsome," the eel said through her gill slits, "when's a charming rat like you going to get married?"

"Very soon, now," he replied, stepping sideways.

He let go of her hand and clasped that of another. This woman was a tall leopard. She moved expertly in the dance.

"Is it you, Eidola?" Piergeiron asked.

"Perhaps, Open Lord," the leopard replied enigmatically. "Perhaps."

He pulled away from her, too. His feet moved faultlessly in the two-step pattern as he circled the room. Sleepwalking. That was what this was. While part of his mind wandered freely, another part, accompanied by his feet, staggered and stumbled, carrying him deeper into nightmare.

Somehow it made sense. The guests were beasts. These monstrous semblances were the faces of their inner selves. Friend and foe alike, they were monsters.

Foes. What foolishness? Shapechanging malaugrym, back-stabbing nobles, plotting guildmasters. As he glided past ogre, beaver, and brownie, Piergeiron wondered if he had a single friend in all the room.

Eidola. She was here somewhere. . . . He would find her.

A pig-headed woman took his hand. No, she was too short and unsure to be Eidola. Next came a puffy fat matron with the head of a hornet. A skeleton, an orc, a fly; a will-o'-the-wisp, a squid, a rooster; a dog, halfling, monkey, tick. . . . Beneath those gray robes moved a multitude of female arms—these too fleshy, these too lean, these too weak, too hairy, too mottled. . . .

Beneath the gold-gilded chandeliers, the details of the masks drifted down robes and arms and legs. Fur, warts, whiskers, rashes, scars, stains, tumors. Every detail of the beasts came alive. They were real. Grotesque creatures glided beside each other in a bizarre menagerie. Alien, hypnotic, menacing, graceful. . . .

A tall, yak-headed woman took his hand. Her doelike brown eyes blinked realistically behind a thin mask of black felt. Her stubbled lips glistened with costume drool. The woman's movements were so lithe within the costume that Piergeiron felt suddenly sure it was Eidola.

A deep-throated purr came from the mask. "I wish I

had known sooner how exquisitely you dance, Lord. You'd not have had a free night in the past year."

Ah, this was his lady love at last. "How about a kiss for the groom?" Piergeiron asked, regaining some of his old spirit.

The yak-woman's eyes opened wide at the invitation, and she ducked her head down. A long yak tongue emerged from between the creature's stumpy yellow teeth and licked wetly across the rat's face.

Piergeiron recoiled. The woman's head was no mask. She was a Zakharan yak-woman, wearing only a small black mask as her costume. She was a real beast.

The Open Lord staggered away from her, gracelessly breaking contact. He glanced dizzily around; nearly half the creatures in this horrific zoo wore small eye masks. Perhaps they, too, were real. Perhaps every last fang, whisker, and horn in the place belonged to real gnolls and wyverns, drakes and sphinxes. Perhaps the staggering, stumbling Open Lord had stepped through the wrong doorway, and this was an infernal and endless dance through the Abyss.

He drifted as if drunk. The dance churned around him. The deadly whirlpool of monsters flung him one way, then another, shouldering him up and dragging him down. . . .

And then, Eidola's hand found his.

"It's you," said the rat-headed paladin.

"At last," came the sharp reply from the lizard-headed woman. "What's wrong with you? Are you drunk?"

Piergeiron shook his head, and his whiskers rattled against boar's teeth. "I'm just flustered. That business with the maidservant and all, and now this dance. . . ."

"Shake it off," Eidola responded. "The maidservant situation was a huge bungle, and it's over. We've got to move ahead. We've got to be ready for midnight."

"Yes," Piergeiron said, still stumbling. "I'll try, but even being near you flusters me."

"Let's get out of this," she suggested. She led him in the dance toward one corner. "The others are waiting."

Piergeiron laughed once, vaguely, searching for some meaning in her words. His misgivings deepened.

Eidola's strong hand pulled him past a gaggle of geese and a line of appraising canines, through a pillared arch, and to a dark cluster of masked creatures.

A sheep turned toward them as they joined the group. "It's about time you two arrived. You'd think you wanted to dance the night away and leave the real danger to the rest of us."

"Shut up. We're here. What news?" snapped the lizard-headed Eidola.

"Nothing new," said the sheep. "The imposter disappeared before the bodyguards could do anything about it. Piergeiron's acting as if nothing's happened, and the ceremony proceeds apace."

"Good," said the lizard. Only then did Piergeiron notice the odd, Calishite burr in her voice.

This was not his bride. This was the leader of a group of conspirators.

Still holding Piergeiron's hand, the woman pushed past the sheep. In one insistent motion, she drew Piergeiron after her and shaped the other six into a circle. She directed the Open Lord into the center of the ring and said,

"Listen, now." To the rat, she commanded harshly, "Report."

The others leaned toward the sewer rat and turned ears of wire mesh and papier-mâché his way.

He muttered, "Well, there isn't much."

"If there isn't much, tell it fast," the woman snapped. "You're wasting time."

He coughed. Masquerading as a noisome rat was difficult enough for the paladin. Doing so when he knew the present company thought him to be someone else was nearly intolerable. But doing all these things and lying atop it all would be too much.

Still, this was a conspiracy. Perhaps he could learn what they were up to by playing along. He would not lie. He would only stall. . . .

"Everything's in place," he said evasively.

The woman's scowl was apparent in her voice. "It's been in place for a tenday, now. Surely you have more than that."

Piergeiron ventured, "The Open Lord suspects something."

"Damn," said the sheep. "I knew it."

"How much does he suspect," the lizard pressed.

"He knows there is a conspiracy."

"Damn, damn," the sheep said. "The whole thing."

"Shut up," the woman advised. "Not the whole thing. Not even the beginning. Of course he knows that much. After the whole fiasco with the maidservant, even the Thickskull could figure out that Eidola was in danger. But what does he know about *us*, about *our* plot? What specifics?"

"What specifics?" asked Piergeiron hopefully.

"*Who* is conspiring. Does he know *who,* and what the plan is?"

"Who?" Piergeiron replied, knowing he was against the wall.

"Us, you idiot," snapped the sheep.

"Well, he suspects you, for one," Piergeiron responded to the sheep. "He is planning to tell the guards to keep an eye on you."

"Damn, damn, damn!" growled the sheep.

"That's it, then," the woman said. "Terr, you're compromised. Check your head at the door and get out of Waterdeep before dawn."

"There's more," Piergeiron ventured, trying to keep the group together. He hoped to steer the conspirators toward a smaller, less-public place, where he could corner them and force them to remove their masks. "But not here. There are too many listening ears. . . ."

"Like these?" the sheep asked, dragging a smallish tiger into the circle. "I thought he'd been listening." He yanked off the head mask to reveal Noph of the family Nesher. The thin nobleman struggled uselessly in the rogue's implacable grip. "Ah, a rich-boy fink. I'll take him with me, slip a knife between his ribs, and dump him in the sewer."

In a rush of hand-stitched fur and gray robe, Piergeiron flung off his costume and was Open Lord once more. Mended peace strings snapped as he drew the long sword. The knight rose to his full, impressive stature and brandished Halcyon threateningly overhead.

"Release young Noph and drop to your knees!" the

Open Lord commanded.

The sheep flung the lad into the belly of Piergeiron and darted for the door.

Piergeiron caught Noph in his free arm and meanwhile swung Halcyon down to block the man's path. The sheep did not stop; nor did the blade. Where they met, sword cleaved through muscle and gut to bone.

In the sudden spray of gore, Piergeiron drew back.

The lizard woman was already gone, as were four of her comrades. Noph flung a hand out to snag the fleeting robe of the last. His fingers caught fabric, not the gray robe but the hem of a red shawl beneath. The conspirator ripped free, unstoppable, and in a single step disappeared among the boiling crowd. Noph suddenly was released from the paladin's grasp. He staggered, falling to his knees and tightly clutching the clue in his hand.

Piergeiron knelt beside the slain man, and both were shadowed beneath Madieron, who had appeared out of nowhere. The pixie held back a gathering crowd.

Piergeiron pulled the sheep's head mask from the dead man. He gazed down at a white, hair-lipped visage with blond curls and a hawkish nose.

"Terrance Decamber—undersecretary to the Master Mariner's Guild," said Piergeiron heavily.

Chapter 3

A Meeting with the Lads

With shapeshifters at large in the castle and nobles and
guildmasters plotting on all sides, Piergeiron could con-
fide in very few. Eidola reduced the possible ranks even
further. She routinely balked at Piergeiron's overprotec-
tiveness, and even now she would certainly forbid him to
enlist the aid of others.

But enlist he would. She did not need to know of her
defenders until she needed their defense—which might
be soon enough.

First, of course, was the inimitable Blackstaff. Khelben was no shapeshifting imposter; the Lord Mage of Waterdeep had a way of dispensing with imitators. He had already been aiding in security; his cursory scans at the gates had turned up plenty of weapons and minor magics. Now Khelben sought much greater and subtler sorceries, the sorts of elaborate wards that usually go undetected. Such protections might hide a shapechanger, or a whole platoon of them. The Lord Mage was even now combing the crowd of guests, servants, and guards.

Next came Madieron Sunderstone. Most shapeshifters could not imitate creatures his size. Even to try, they would have to overcome the blond-haired man-mountain—no small feat. Besides, the man's combination of dull wits and deep wisdom would defy duplication. Piergeiron was confident that the Madieron who had greeted him in his apartments this morning was the same man who stood by him now—and would stay at his side until he met Eidola at the altar.

Then, there was Captain Rulathon, Piergeiron's second-in-command of the city watch. This black mustachioed warrior was no imitation, either, for Khelben himself had teleported him in for the briefing. His expertise at subtle reconnaissance was matched only by his knowledge of the folk of Waterdeep. Few impostors could sneak past him.

And, last—Noph Nesher. No shapeshifter would have thought to take his form, and the noble youth had already proved his worth. He had eavesdropped on various conspirators and had gathered the first hard evidence—a bit of fabric torn from one of them.

Piergeiron, Madieron, Rulathon, and Noph met in a

small vestibule off the palace kitchens. It was just the sort of unfinished and unwelcoming space that often hatched conspiracies, whispered plans that would shake continents.

Rulathon listened closely, his black hair flaring wildly about his intent face. Noph tried to look equally focused, though a thin film of sweat glistened on his white brow. Madieron's expression was ponderous and a bit vacant amid the dark and rough-hewn rafters.

The Open Lord recounted what he had learned from the conspirators. "There is treason in it. It is no simple matter of impersonating a maid or whispers in the corners. It is a kidnapping plot, or assassination, or some such. And as yet, I still do not know who precisely is behind it all. At best, the shapeshifters are chaotic creatures working on their own, and December was acting outside the orders of the mariners. At worst, these conspiracies might reach deep into the ranks of Waterdeep's nobles and guilds."

"The mariners have plenty of reasons to block an overland trade route," Captain Rulathon noted grimly.

"Yes," agreed Piergeiron," but so would many other folk. Whoever is behind it all, I am convinced that the trade route to Kara-Tur is key."

"I came to the same conclusion," Noph interrupted. The other three turned their attention on him, as he smiled sheepishly. "It's where the money leads. Somebody wants to prevent the signing of the pact—prevent it or control it. I personally suspect the Master Mariners above all others."

Piergeiron regarded the youth keenly. "Even if there weren't shapeshifters running amok," he said, "I would have had to be very selective in whom I put my trust. Out of all Waterdeep, I have selected you three, and Khelben."

"But any of us could be . . ." Noph began. He broke off with the shaking of Captain Rulathon's head.

"Be assured we are not, son," said the watchcaptain. "Be assured and be glad. Our forms may not have been stolen from us yet, but watch out! I imagine that before the night is through, we will be running into ourselves walking down the hall, or fighting ourselves on some stair somewhere."

Noph swallowed loudly, simultaneously relieved and dismayed.

Piergeiron picked up the thread of the discussion. "I need each of you, my ears and eyes where I cannot be. Rulathon, first and foremost, you must guard my bride and see that no harm comes to her. Noph, you must watch the guests for telltale signs of treason. Madieron, of course, will be watching me. Khelben is already at work, scanning the crowd. All of you have been doing these things. Now I make your commissions official."

The Open Lord paused. A wave of exhaustion, unexpected, swept over him. "Friends, this is a maze from which Eidola and I cannot escape alone. With plots upon plots upon plots, perhaps we will not survive, even with your aid."

"So you will still marry Eidola tonight?" Captain Rulathon asked.

"I will," Piergeiron replied, resolute. "Whatever these plots, they are wrapped up in the wedding and in this trade route. The conspirators' work would already be done if I canceled the ceremony now."

"I imagine your bride is of like mind," said the captain. He turned. "Perhaps I should make certain of it." Bowing once in farewell, he headed away, toward Eidola's chambers. "I go to watch."

"Good," Piergeiron said. His very serious gaze spoke a silent thanks to the tall warrior.

Then Piergeiron turned those same eyes—those that had gazed into the abyss of Undermountain and across at the glorious panoply of Waterdeep—upon Noph. "Rulathon's work is begun—and Madieron's and Khelben's, also. I count on yours, too. If you help Eidola and me win our way out of these traps, the whole of Waterdeep will owe you a debt of gratitude."

The lad nodded seriously. In respectful imitation of Rulathon, he said, "I go to watch." Noph turned and slipped away down the hall, toward the sounds of dancing.

* * * * *

"Your autographs here, Gentles," said the Open Lord of Waterdeep.

He leaned over his large mahogany desk and placed the much-signed trade pact before the last holdout delegates: the Boarskyrs.

The two red-faced and burly brothers, Becil and Bullard, had inherited title and lands from a great-great-great-great-grandfather Boarskyr—the man who'd built the first Boarskyr bridge. Each succeeding generation that descended from this extraordinary man, though, had lost another "great." Becil and Bullard were the inevitable result. They could not be truthfully called good, let alone great.

The brothers had not inherited their ancestor's enterprising spirit or even his common sense. Uneducated and mired in penury, Becil and Bullard could use the opportunity and money the trade route would bring them. Unfortunately, they liked their backward backwater and wanted to keep it as it was. Perhaps it was the only place they truly fit in.

Here, in Piergeiron's cherry wood-paneled study, the two looked and smelled as out of place and nervous as sheepdogs caught in the slaughter chute.

Their mood was not helped by Madieron's looming presence and his unscheduled groans of disapproval.

"Look here, Your Fecundity, Laird Pallid," began Becil, the slightly redder, burlier, and more verbal of the brothers.

"*Lord Paladinson* will suffice," corrected the Open Lord gently.

"Look here, Laird Pallidson," Becil continued, "we've got a histrionical and advantageous bridge—that's sure. You've got a compounded interest in it—that's sure, too. And, if it comes to it, Your Feckless Personage is asked to cross our bridge whensoever that you as an individuality would like to do so, as would make us indeed felicitatiously happy. Really."

"Thank you very much."

Bullard interrupted, "How about I have a look at your sword?"

"How about you let us finish our business first?" Piergeiron replied.

"But as to Your Immensity going off and inviting the rest of the world to circumnavigate our bridge," Becil continued obliviously, "well, now that's a pickle. And, you know, even an Enormous Egregiousness like yourself can make a pickle from a cucumber but not a cucumber from a pickle, apples and peach pits marching to a different kettle of fish altogether, if you follow my thinking."

"I do not."

Bullard scooted his chair to one side of Piergeiron's desk, and then pretended to be intensely interested in a corner of the ceiling. His feverish eyes slipped for a moment down to Piergeiron's long sword, and his fingers twiddled in anticipation.

Madieron's own fingers did a little twiddling.

"Well, for one thing," Becil prattled on, "it's not so great a bridge, Your Obesity. I'd say even with you and that pony of yours—Deadheart, is it?—

"Dreadnought."

"—Deadweight, right, thanking Your Monstrosity, well, that much weighty preponderance might make the whole thing go over into the river. Then we'd not have our hysterical and advantageous bridge and you'd not have your compounded interest, neither. You see, my brother Bullard was the archipelago of the current edifice, and just because he's got piles doesn't mean he knows about pilings. . . ."

"I'd hold my tongue, Becil—" Bullard advised as he shifted his chair around beside Piergeiron.

"I'm sure our heiratic bridge would break under Your Ponderous Propensity and your pony, Dreadlocks, not to mention your bodyguard Matterhorn—"

Madieron growled, splitting his disapproval equally between the brothers.

Into the tense silence that followed this vocalization, Piergeiron ventured, "The agreement allows for a whole new bridge, one you two wouldn't need to build yourselves. And the bridge would have a toll, to enrich your family into perpetuity." Piergeiron thought but didn't add that they could and should use that toll for educating future Boarskyrs.

"But like we extrapolated," Becil continued, "we could care less about the future. We could care more about the present."

"Once you go changing the present, all you've got left is the future," Bullard noted, nodding enthusiastically. "By the way, how about I get a look at your sword?"

Madieron folded his arms over his chest and let out an unappreciative hiss.

"No," Piergeiron reiterated. He turned to Becil. "You said you would sign."

"We said we'd *not* sign," Becil corrected, "*until* you'd been nuptualized to Eidola of Neverwinter—"

"—our kin."

"—and with kin of ours ruling Waterdeep—through the allspices of Yours Truly (no, I mean Yours Truly as in *Yours* Truly, not Mine Truly)—we know you will promulgate a present-tense orientational direction for our little village, Great High Commissary."

If ever the mouse held the elephant at bay, thought Piergeiron. . . .

He said with a bit more exasperation than he had intended, "But I *am* marrying her!"

"You're not married yet," Becil pointed out.

Madieron released a moan that sounded as though it

came from a tree on the brink of toppling.

Piergeiron felt a sudden insistent tugging at his sword-belt.

"Peace strings!" Bullard proclaimed angrily where he yanked on the hilt of Halcyon. He was about to brace a foot on Piergeiron's back, but Madieron's own foot removed the man as though he were a dog and Halcyon an unappreciative leg.

As Bullard tumbled to the floor, he said, with no sign of rancor. "Until the Brothers Borskyr see gold on your finger, you won't be seeing their Xs on your paper."

"A lot can happen between here and the altar—the viscerals of life in the big city," Becil said. "No ring, no sign."

"How about I have a look at that sword—"

"No!" shouted Piergeiron and Madieron in chorus.

Becil slapped his brother's hand away, whereupon the unflappable Bullard flapped. "Hands off, Im-Becil."

"Im-Becil," murmured Madieron, and he chuckled to himself. "I get it. Im-Becil."

"Shut up, Dullard!"

"Im-Becil and Dullard," Madieron repeated, chortling.

As the blond giant laughed and the Boarskyr Brothers engaged in a spirited slap-fight, Piergeiron thought once again about building a five-mile loop around Boarskyr Bridge and letting the town wither to nothing in the shadow of the great caravan way. Still, Grandfather Boarskyr had built in the best spot for fifty miles up or down the river. Circumventing it would be more costly, more time consuming, and more galling than even these negotiations.

The Open Lord's musings were interrupted by Bullard, who was seated and therefore had won the fight. "After all, Laird Pallidson, we didn't become Boarskyrs by being idiots."

Piergeiron couldn't help himself. "You became idiots by being Boarskyrs."

Red-cheeked, Becil struggled up from the floor. He regarded his brother darkly. "Pinky flicker."

"How about I have a look at that sword?"

"Dullard, ha ha," Madieron said, struggling to squelch his giggles. "Ha ha."

* * * * *

When Eidola emerged from her latest session beneath the sharp-nailed fingers of hairdressers and face powderers, Captain Rulathon was waiting. He merged more deeply with the shadows of the hallway. His always-intent face was especially grave.

The watchcaptain was not blind to Eidola's beauty. Her gown was exquisite, her makeup flawless. The fortress of hair, flowers, lace, and pins atop her head was a construct worthy of any siege engineer. The gem that hung from a silver chain round her slender throat glowed and sparkled in the candlelight.

Yes, she is beautiful, Rulathon thought, but artificially so. She is cold calculation instead of warm wildflowers. Every face she stares into is a mirror. When she seems to gaze lovingly into Piergeiron's eyes, she admires only her own reflection.

Beside and behind Eidola came a flock of chattering

manicurists and hairdressers—the attendants who had worked the magic over her. They were each garbed in the ceremonial satins and laces that marked them as the retinue of the bride, though the ivory shade of their dresses showed that they lacked her white virtue. The women pranced and laughed excitedly as they moved along.

In a shimmering rush, they were past. Rulathon waited a breath before he started out from the recess. A frisson of intuition ran up his spine, and he drew back. A last attendant came scuttling up behind. She called out for the others to wait and ran on toward their oblivious backs.

As she flapped past, the watchcaptain thought for a moment he glimpsed, beneath the ruffle of skirts, a trailing tentacle.

A tentacle, he thought. One would think a hairdresser would know enough to tuck away so telltale a thing.

He stepped from the crevice, and pursued them through the darkness of the corridor.

* * * * *

Just before the wedding ceremony began, Noph cornered Jheldarr "Stormrunner" Boaldegg, First Mariner of the Master Mariners' Guild. The sea dog stood in the narthex of the palace chapel, and like the other guests, waited to be seated for the ceremony.

Noph casually approached the man. "An honest to goodness sea captain," he said admiringly.

The old seaman stared out from behind a fleecy white mask of beard and eyebrows. Around a battered pipe, he drawled, "Aye."

"This is the closest I've ever been to real adventure," Noph pressed. "As the son of a nobleman, I read plenty of stories of the briny deep, but have never gotten to sail out on it myself."

"Aye."

Noph's demeanor suddenly changed from casual excitement to focused desire. "I want to go to sea."

Captain Boaldegg fixed him with a stern look.

"I wouldn't need a commission," Noph said quietly, all the while glancing over his shoulder. "I know you give officer commissions to some nobles—but I'd be willing to holystone decks and haul sheets."

The white-bearded sea dog blinked in consideration, his scarred red face looking for all the world like a hunk of granite. At last, he let go the blue pipe smoke he'd held in his lungs and said, "Deck hands are abundant. We've got plenty of them straight from jails and flophouses. They don't ask much pay, try to avoid trouble, and know their trade. Why should I bump one of them seasoned seamen to take on a load of noble trouble?"

"Trouble?" asked Noph in an injured tone. "I wouldn't make any trouble. Besides, I heard there's going to be need for plenty more hands once . . . once the trade pact falls through."

Though before, the seaman's eyes had seemed glassy and amused beneath his eyebrows, now they were sharp as arrowheads. "What makes you think the pact is jeopardized, lad?"

Noph returned the man's steely glare. "I know about what you have planned. I know about . . . Eidola."

Suddenly, the man's old hand—steel bars and cables—seized Noph's arm. "You're coming with me, lad."

"Oh, no he's not," interrupted Laskar Nesher. From behind his son, he pried the captain's hand loose. "No son of mine—no *heir* of mine—is going to waste his life with a bunch of thieves and bilge rats. Get gone, old Boaldegg. Troll the gutters and prisons for your shipmates."

With that, Laskar Nesher drew his son away from the glowering sea dog. For once, the merchant's eyes were focused on his son—focused and intent. "What's this all about, Kastonoph?"

"You wouldn't understand," Noph said truthfully.

Laskar managed to look angered, hurt, and understanding, all at once. He gripped his son's arm harder than had the captain and dragged Noph to the relative privacy of the crying room, behind the narthex.

"I know you think me a copper-coddling miser, a fool preoccupied with the flash of coins and unable to see true riches," said the man earnestly. His eyes were feverishly bright. "I often think so, myself. But the reason for it all is that I'm trying to build a dynasty for you. Yes, I am a fool. In the process of amassing a fortune, I've made you despise anything you might inherit from me."

"It's all right, Father," began Noph. "You don't have to—"

"But don't give up on me now, Son. At last, my frugality has paid off, has put me in a place where everything will change for us. And it is all wrapped up in this wedding, in the Lady Eidola herself."

The nobleman paused, expecting another interruption, but Noph was as silent and still as a statue.

Laskar gingerly began again, as if poking at a wound. "I have certain . . . information about the Lady Eidola—about her past . . . information she desperately wants to keep from her husband."

"Father," said Noph in alarm. The momentary empathy he had felt for the man fled. "Blackmail? Is this the future you have planned for me?"

"Don't think of it as blackmail. I'm not asking her for money—just for the assurance of work. There's going to be lots of wood needed for bridges and corduroy roads once this trade pact is finished, and I want us to supply that wood."

Noph's usually white face was now blotched with red—disappointment and, worse, pity. "What have you become? You'd commit extortion? And against the Lady Eidola?"

"It isn't extortion," his father blustered. "We'll be working for every copper we make off this. And if you knew about her what I know—"

"Enough!" cried Noph in a sudden rage. "I can't stomach another word from you. I can't stand to breathe the same air as you." Laskar tried to interrupt, but Noph swept his hand up before the man "Speak, and I will empty my stomach on you, I swear it. You nauseate me. I nauseate me—the very fact that I am your son makes me sick. Let it be punishment enough that I have inherited your looks—do not add the burden of your deceits."

He turned and stalked back toward the narthex, where guests were lined up to be shown to their seats. At the arched entrance to the crying room, he said, "I hope you have enough honor to disown me." And with that, he left.

Noph growled inwardly. No, his father was not in league with the malaugrym or the mariners, or anyone else seeking to stop the wedding. No, his father was not a traitor or a murderer. Laskar Nesher was merely a petty criminal in times that called men to greatness.

Father has chosen his own road, Noph thought. I need to do the same.

"Sir, your name?" asked the liveried attendant by the door.

Noph hesitated, unsure what to say. At last, he murmured, "Put me down simply as Freeman Kastonoph, friend and loyal servant of the groom."

Interlude:

The Silver Margin

Midnight has come.
The time for worry about plots is done.
Let the traitors do their worst.
They will have to reckon with me.
They will have to fight Madieron and Captain Rulathon.
The Blackstaff guards us, too, and even young Kastonoph.
Whatever comes, I will marry Eidola; the Boarskyrs

will sign the pact; all the world will be forever changed.

For better or for worse.

I am already dizzy with change.

I cling to the wooden chancel screen, fashioned of burled walnut. Walnut has its swirls. Disease twists these into burls. We carve the burls into flourishes and filigree.

One chaos is carved from another.

I gaze through the screen. The chapel is carved into pieces by it.

I see fragments of a bright, crowded sanctuary. I see dark pieces of the gathered guests. I see empty sections of blackness where my bride will appear.

Fragments and pieces . . .

Rock to sand to dust to nothing at all. . . .

The sanctuary is slowly listing over.

It will capsize before my bride stands beside me.

We will be married on the ceiling.

Cold sweat stands on my white cheeks. I am glad Sandrew gave me this bucket.

I see a piece of my young spy. Noph strides solemnly through the screen spaces. He fits himself onto an already loaded bench.

There is something different about him. His swagger is gone. Even he is changed. He suddenly seems a man.

"Tomorrow, I am a man."

I spoke those words long, long ago. The memory is as strong and stinging as distilled spirits.

Shaleen is a silhouette against the dim gloaming.

She stands framed by a rugged wood doorway. Beyond her hangs a hay hook. It is tangled with its block and tackle. The barn slats glow with predawn.

I rise. Hay drops from me. I shiver, feeling the cold against my bare skin. I shiver again, with something else.

This is a mistake. Nothing will be the same now. Nothing. She will forever be different. I, too. A yearning shoots through me. I wish to return to the day before, to our young and simple lives.

I search in the hay for my breeches. The sound of my hand is loud in the morning.

"Come here," Shaleen whispers.

I look up to her. She stands there, bare as the morning.

"Come see."

I nod. I try to rise, but my legs tremble. The loft's planks are rough under my feet.

I reach her.

She, too, trembles, but her shoulders and back are warm and solid in the darkness.

"Look," she says. Her hand points outward.

Beyond the turbulence of the autumn forest, a slim curtain rises in the night. It is the silver margin between dark and day. "Tomorrow."

The sound of that single word makes my heart break.

"Tomorrow," I echo.

Apologies and fears well up inside me, but no words. There is only gushing emotion—shame, longing, regret, passion, hopelessness. . . .

"Tomorrow, I am a woman," Shaleen says.

She nestles against me. At her touch, the dread and fear amalgamate into something greater, something new. My trembling stops. I draw a long, contented breath.

"Tomorrow, I am a man."

The music begins, unstoppable.

The trump sounds.

The drums cadence like thunder.

The fragmented sanctuary returns around me.

I am dizzy.

I am lost, here in my own palace, my own wedding, my own life.

It *is* tomorrow.

Everything has changed, for better or for worse.

Chapter 4

What Once Bound All To All

The sanctuary glowed with the light of a thousand
candles.

They stood ensconced along the limestone walls. They
topped candle stands, lit aisles, and flickered in votive
constellations at the feet of statued heroes. They bathed
everything at the human level in suffused light, but left the
heads of the statues, the vault above, and every other
heavenly thing in darkness.

Benches of black walnut bent ever so slightly beneath the burden of nobles, guildmasters, ambassadors. The sanctuary was full, and only half the guests had been seated. The others would stand in the narthex, craning to hear and see.

Pipes, trumpets, and drums blasted out the bridal march. The ceremony had begun.

* * * * *

It was too late to stop the shapeshifters.

By the time Captain Rulathon had found Khelben in the wedding crowd and warned him that one or all of the bride's attendants were shapeshifters, Eidola was walking down the sanctuary aisle.

Khelben cast quick magics to win past the elaborate wards that masked the women.

"You are right. She is accompanied by eight monsters," said the Lord Mage of Waterdeep, incredulously watching the attendants sashay down the aisle.

The shapeshifters glided along beside the bride. None was more than a claw's length away from her, a breath away from their prey.

"What do we do?" Rulathon whispered. "Can't you flash them all away into sifting soot?"

Khelben grimaced. "No. They are too close to the bride, and the guests. Still, we might have a chance if. . . ." His words fell to mutterings.

Rulathon gazed intently at the mage's face.

"It's a long walk up the aisle, girls," Khelben thought aloud. "If I can't beat you, I may as well join you. . . ."

He murmured something else and swept an arcane gesture down his torso. With a pop that was barely audible over the pipes and trumpets, the black-robed and gray-bearded mage was replaced by a slim, ivory-garbed attendant.

The lass gave Rulathon a very Khelbenesque wink. She hurried forward, her stride somewhat more businesslike and determined than those of her comrades. She caught up to the smiling cluster and began her own smile.

It was a toothy grimace. Through it came a growled warning, magically sounding in the ears of the attendants:

Hello, shapeshifters. This is the Blackstaff speaking to you. Congratulations for living this long. Stay in your current forms and fall back behind the bride's train, and you will live longer, still.

There was no sign that the creatures had heard him, except that their pace slackened. Eidola moved forward, out of arm's reach.

Unfortunately, thought Khelben, shapeshifters have a knack for growing things longer than arms.

Very good, Sisters, the Blackstaff hissed to them. *You've no doubt felt the spell blades I've conjured within your bellies. As long as you make no sudden moves and stay in your current forms, those daggers probably won't cut anything vital.*

The pace of the party slowed even more.

Khelben's smile deepened.

Now, let's chat about who you are and what you are doing here. Piergeiron thinks you are malaugrym. I have a notion you are somewhat worse. Am I right?

Eight coiffured heads nodded on their lovely necks.

I thought so. And as to what that something is . . . let's repair to the crying room for a little talk. . . .

* * * * *

Bagpipes shrieked their solemn songs, drummers cracked sticks against skins, corpulent and decadent nobles turned about in their seats to gawk at the spectacle of flower-decked maidens and flag bearers. The bride and her attendants glided down the aisle. Benches groaned when Waterdeep's powers-that-be rose on their own legs to nod benevolently. . . .

Standing among them, Noph saw his father a few rows back. Laskar's sycophantic smile was worst of all. His teeth seemed to spell out the word *blackmail*.

Noph felt ill. He looked away from his erstwhile father, and also from the bride. Her secret past, whatever it was, made her white gown a travesty. Surely there was someplace in the sanctuary he could stare without getting sick.

The Eye of Ao. The ancient panel of stained glass hung high in the wall above the chancel. The huge eye was a splendid piece of craftsmanship, backlit by a loft of flickering candles. The eye was luminous, alive. Even its pupil glinted with capricious light.

Its pupil? The Eye of Ao was supposed to have an empty pupil. The hole symbolized the place of dark mysteries through which all mortals flew after death.

How could an empty space reflect light?

Then Noph saw: the triangular glint of light came from an arrowhead poised in the opening.

"Damn," Noph swore aloud.

The nobles around him turned and glared. Noph turned the curse into a cough. The guests blinked and looked away. Noph continued coughing, sputtering, gagging. He pulled out a kerchief and tried unsuccessfully to contain the fit.

"Excuse me," he muttered hoarsely, and pushed his way toward the side aisle.

Nobles happily let him pass, some shying from him as though he carried a plague. In moments, Noph was free. He hurried down the side aisle toward the nearest door. It led to a set of stairs going up.

Noph bolted up the stairs, hoping he could find his way to the Eye of Ao before Lady Eidola flew through it in death.

* * * * *

Piergeiron stood uneasily at the front of the sanctuary and watched his bride approach. She moved with constant, stately grace. The smile on her face seemed one part joy and one part wry discomfort. He wondered if she felt as troubled as he. . . .

Something was very wrong here. Piergeiron could not dismiss the dizzy dread. It was almost unbearable. Worst of all, he could do nothing to combat it. He could only stand, smile distressedly, and hope—hope that whatever plots had been hatched would fail, or would not come into being until he and Eidola were lawfully wed.

Beyond Eidola, her attendants slowed and stopped. They curtseyed once, their bodies rigidly upright, and began to back slowly away.

Where were they going? They were supposed to accompany Eidola to the altar. Did they back away because of some terrible danger about to descend on her?

Piergeiron glanced up into the black vault, unseeable above his bride. Were those leathery wings? Was that a lashing tail? No, he thought, only shadow play, only particles swimming in my eyes.

Piergeiron steadied himself and looked back down, all the while wondering what invisible monsters of fate hovered above them, ready to descend.

The martial cadence of the bagpipes slowed. Eidola took two final steps and stood beside him. The roar of trumpets and drums ceased and echoed away.

Bride and groom turned to face the podium that held Sandrew, the Savant of Oghma. He gestured for the people to be seated. As the muffled sound of creaking benches settled into silence, he spoke:

"Friends, we are here to witness a union that will mean joy and peace for all of us, but especially for this man and this woman."

I only hope he is right about that, thought Piergeiron. I could use a few lifetimes of peace just now. . . .

* * * * *

Noph at last topped the ladder and gently lifted the trapdoor above him.

"Found it," he whispered to himself.

Beyond the trapdoor was a small, candlelit loft. Its far wall was the stained-glass Eye of Ao. Countless candles lined the base of the Eye, and fire gleamed in its edges.

Through the huge pupil came the murmurous sound of Sandrew's homily on marriage.

On this side of the pupil, though, was a cocked crossbow poised on a wooden stand. Its quarrel was trained downward, pointing to the spot where Eidola and Piergeiron stood.

Noph almost flung wide the trapdoor and rushed in, but he noticed a string tied to the door. It was threaded through an eyelet in the floor and then rose up to the trigger of the crossbow. He eased the door downward an inch, and watched as the quivering line loosened. The trigger settled back in its place.

Clever. Whoever had placed this crossbow here had rigged it to go off if the trapdoor was opened. Cleverer, still, there was another string attached to the trigger. It was tied to a clockwork mechanism. As Noph watched, the string wound slowly around the clock spindle, and the trigger tightened.

"... *The crossbow is already in place*. ..."

So, even now, the lizard-woman is conspicuously sitting in the crowd, thought Noph, with a solid alibi for the moment when the quarrel flies and the lady or the lord is slain. ...

He had another minute at most—a minute to cut the first string, climb into the loft, and cut the second.

He reached for his dagger and pulled it forth—or tried to. The peace strings held the damned thing in place. He yanked harder, but he didn't have the strength of a Piergeiron to snap them. Groaning in frustration, Noph fiddled for a moment more, trying to untie the tangle.

Thirty seconds ... The clockwork string tightened. ...

Noph reached up past the trapdoor, feeling for where the first line was attached. His hand followed the string to another eyelet that was screwed into the top of the door. A yank on the eyelet told him this knot was secure.

Nineteen seconds . . .

Noph gingerly rolled his fingertips across the string, his nails slowly fraying the fibers apart.

Eight seconds . . .

A grunt and a yank. The frayed string broke loose of the eyelet. Noph flung back the trapdoor. It boomed loudly, but he did not care.

Two seconds . . . The crossbow trigger drew back, trembling.

Noph lunged for the clockwork mechanism. A crooked nail in the floorboards caught his toe, and he fell.

One second . . . The trigger clicked. . . .

Noph snatched the base of the crossbow stand and wrenched it. The quarrel shot away. It pinged off the edge of Ao's pupil and darted down into the crowd. A woman's scream came up to him, followed by the shout of a man. Noph leapt to his feet and peered out the pupil. Below, an old dowager clutched a bleeding arm.

The bolt had missed Lady Eidola and Piergeiron. They were safe.

"The whole of Waterdeep will owe you a debt of gratitude."

Except that Waterdeep had confused the details. . . .

Someone pointed up toward the Eye of Ao and shouted: "Assassin!"

Noph went white. As other faces turned toward him, he backed away into the dark chamber. He was no assassin.

He was the hero who stopped the murderers. Once the people saw the evidence . . . once they saw the stand and the strings and clockwork mechanism, they would understand the truth. . . .

The cries of the congregation were interrupted by the hiss of a line of smokepowder, lit by the candles beneath the eye.

Smokepowder?

Boom!

Searing heat. Noph was thrown against a very hard wall. He groaned and crumpled amid orange flames. They died back as quickly as they had come. Bleeding, Noph struggled to smother the fire on his cape.

Numbly, he realized what had happened. The woman who had set up the crossbow had trapped it to explode once it had gone off, destroying the evidence of her crime, destroying the evidence of Noph's innocence.

Crossbow, stand, and clockwork machine had been blasted apart.

"Assassin! Assassin!" came the cries from below.

Chapter 5
Where Trust Is Placed

"Assassin!"

Piergeiron clutched Eidola protectively to him and looked up toward the Eye of Ao. The crossbow bolt had come from there. In the pupil of the Eye was the frightened, hopeful face of young Noph.

The Open Lord's heart sank. What treachery was this?

Noph backed quickly away, turning to flee.

"Guards!" called Piergeiron. "To the Eye of Ao!"

His command was interrupted when the Eye flared brilliantly, as though it had ceased to be stained glass and had become the very flesh and soul of a god. Fire shot out through the pupil, jetting twenty feet into the sanctuary.

Piergeiron clutched his bride all the more tightly as the holocaust roared overhead. He saw their shadows, cast downward by the bright blast—an image malformed and monstrous.

Then the blast, too, was gone. Piergeiron looked up to see a charred Eye of Ao, black smoke bleeding up into the caliginous vault above. He stepped away from his bride and drew Halcyon for the third time that day.

"Forgive me, Eidola, but the duties of office call," Piergeiron said, bowing to kiss her hand.

Already, sounds of struggle came from the Eye of Ao; the guards had reached the would-be assassin. Kern and Miltiades rushed toward the sounds, swords unsheathed. Piergeiron looked the other way, where men carried away the wounded dowager.

He shrugged, "Perhaps my aid won't be needed, after all."

"Got him!" shouted someone in the Eye. "We got him!"

During all this commotion, Sandrew, the Savant of Oghma, had remained unflappable. "Shall I continue?"

Hushed flashes and muffled booms suddenly came from the crying room at the far end of the sanctuary. Screams answered, and more flares, and a man's angry voice shouting arcane words. Guests standing in the narthex shied back from the sounds.

A smoldering door barked open and spilled flames out into the rear of the sanctuary. A gasp ran through the chapel. Guests scrambled over each other to get out of the way. A tattered and smoky Khelben Arunsun staggered out through the opening and stopped to cough violently.

"Khelben looks to need some aid," Piergeiron noted mildly to Eidola.

She was apparently in complete agreement, for she had already turned to dart down the aisle, dragging the groom after her. Piergeiron had to step lively to keep from getting tangled in her train.

They were halfway to the Lord Mage when lightning jabbed from the doorway, struck him, glowed along hair and teeth and bones, and flashed him away to smoke and ash.

Wide-eyed, Piergeiron and Eidola ran all the faster. Guards converged on the smoky scene.

Another Khelben fell out through the door, his robes ablaze. The guards halted, stunned. One young soldier rushed in to pat out the flames. He, too, leapt back as a fireball roared into being atop the writhing form.

Khelben was toasted, yet again. . . .

"What is this?" Piergeiron shouted to his running bride.

A third and fourth Khelben rushed from the crying room. These two clasped hands and barged past the stunned guards, dropping them to the floor. A whirling swarm of magic missiles spun out the doorway, shot past the guards, and pelted through the fleeing Blackstaffs. Light blazed within, and the two, still holding hands, fell in a burning heap together.

The fifth Khelben emerged from the crying room just as Eidola and Piergeiron fought their way through a stampede of guests fleeing up the aisle. Piergeiron pushed ahead of Eidola and raised his sword.

"Hurl no more magics!" the Open Lord commanded.

The latest Khelben cocked a hairy brow at him. "That would be inconvenient, just now." He turned and flung out his fingers. A mystic hand appeared before the door, and into it two more Khelbens charged. The hand closed on them and squeezed, crushing flesh, bone, fabric, and magic.

"I said, hold!" cried Piergeiron. He rushed up behind the master mage and slid Halcyon beneath his neck.

"I suppose you did," replied the fifth Khelben. Cautiously, he raised his hands up into the air. "But there is one more of me coming. You'll have to tell him, too."

A ninth Khelben darted from the door, halted in shock as the guards caught him, looked around at the tableau of drifting ash and dripping flesh, and snarled, "Unhand me!"

The guards did. The mage straightened his rumpled black robes and glared at Piergeiron. "Nice of you to get involved."

The Open Lord said, "Guards, slay that man if he makes so much as a sorcerous twitch." The guards moved into position to do so. "Good. Now, what is happening here?"

"Shapeshifters," the Khelbens replied in unison. The fifth fell silent in Piergeiron's grasp as the ninth explained. "Somehow they disposed of Lady Eidola's attendants and took their places. When I found them out, I led them back into the crying room for questioning. One of them attacked. They rushed for the door, taking my form to confuse pursuit."

"If I am a shapeshifter," said the fifth, "why did I slay two of my comrades with a crushing hand?"

The ninth shook his head. "He slew only those two, and in front of you so that you would believe him. I killed the rest."

"A crushing hand is no easy spell, Open Lord," said the fifth.

"Many shapeshifters know magic," the ninth replied. "Your casting is no proof of your identity."

Piergeiron ground his teeth together. "This is like blind-fighting. I'm as likely to kill friend as foe."

"Wouldn't it be better, Open Lord," said the fifth, "to let a shapechanger free than to accidentally slay the Lord Mage of Waterdeep?"

He was right. Piergeiron released his hold on the fifth Khelben.

The mage staggered free, huffed, and then struggled to straighten his robes. He glanced up in irritation at Piergeiron. "Thanks for the rough treatment. I have half a mind—"

Then, absurdly, his words were literally true. His head split down the middle and fountained red upon all those around. The Open Lord reeled back in surprise and revulsion, and the body slumped to the floor.

Eidola pulled back from the slain form, the sword in her hand dripping gore. She looked as surprised by her action as did everyone else. Her wedding dress was painted in crimson, and her hands trembled.

"You were quite right," said the ninth Khelben, stepping toward her. "You knew I would never try to save myself at the peril of the city. Gentles, if you would put away your swords—"

"Wait!" shouted Piergeiron. "We still have no proof."

Eidola gave him a look of injured pride.

Piergeiron thought of all those in whom he had placed his trust—Noph, who turned out to be an assassin; Khelben, who was eight parts shapeshifter to one part master mage; and beautiful, mysterious Eidola, the spirit and image of long-gone Shaleen.

"Put away your swords," the Open Lord said, lowering his blade. "The judgment of my bride is proof enough."

"That's good," said the Blackstaff. "The monster she just slew would concur." He gestured toward the riven head and body before them.

They all saw it, then. The body had returned to its true appearance—a gray-hided humanoid creature with huge eyes and a broad, spiky head.

"A doppleganger?" the Open Lord gasped.

"So it would seem," said Khelben, prodding the thing with an iron-toed boot. "Not malaugrym, but dopplegangers."

"But why?" asked Piergeiron. He turned to his bride and clutched her hand. "To kill Eidola?"

"I doubt it," Khelben said dryly, shaking his head. "They could have killed her a hundred times before now. Besides, as our young friend Noph has shown, there are much easier ways to assassinate a lady."

"But if not to kill her," Piergeiron asked, "then why?"

Khelben cocked a knowing eyebrow at the bride and said, "That very simple question will take, I am afraid, a very long time to puzzle out." He cast his gaze outward at the stone-silent crowd, many of whom stood with candlesticks and snuffers and other improvised weapons in hand. "And this is neither the time nor place for such riddles."

With a wave of Khelben's hand, Eidola's dress, make-up, and hair were once again in perfect order. She looked admiringly at herself, then glanced at her groom to see that he, also, had been made over.

Khelben addressed the crowd, "I fear I haven't spells for all of you, so tuck in those shirttails, straighten those gowns, and lick back those bangs. We've a wedding to celebrate!"

A wondering murmur circulated among the crowd.

"Music!" called Khelben.

The trumpets responded first, once again taking up the bridal march. The drums added their cadence, and the bagpipes growled to life.

Khelben motioned to the guards to remove the body and clean up the soot. They flinched at first from his flicking fingers, but then busied themselves about their tasks.

Arm in arm, bride and groom headed down the aisle, striding to the martial strains of the wedding march. In waves, the crowd shook off its stunned silence and straightened its collective cummerbund. It even mustered a smile for the wedding couple.

Piergeiron tried to return the smile, but couldn't.

He couldn't breathe.

He couldn't stop swallowing.

His head felt like a papier-mâché mask.

Oh, to sleep. . . .

This dread. This mourning. He had not felt such anguish since the night Shaleen had died. The image of his first wife again rose before him, filled his vision.

Oh, to sleep. . . .

The candles all through the sanctuary abruptly flared to life. Their flames leapt up six feet into the air. The congregation cowered away from this new assault, and the trumpets and drums faltered into silence. In the agonized dying of the bagpipes came human shrieks—

Fiery figures formed in the flaring candles: warriors, dressed in armor, their swords drawn.

With a final flash, the flaming beings became solid flesh. They dropped to the floor. With them descended a heavy, preternatural night.

Chapter 6
Blind Fighting

This is not the end, thought Noph, not by a long shot.

He had begun the evening a disaffected young noble. Judging by others of his breed, he had been clearly destined to become a jaded and decadent middle-aged noble. But something had happened along the way. Somehow he'd caught a glimpse of what he was going to be and had boldly worked to change it all.

He had decided to be a hero.

Why, then, was he imprisoned in a dungeon cell, awaiting trial and execution as an assassin?

He had heard that such was often the lot of heroes—to be misunderstood and branded villains. Only now did it occur to him just how galling was such a fate. He had been disowned by his father, had risked his skin to save Lord Piergeiron and Lady Eidola, and at the end of it all, had been labeled a monster.

"Some hero I turned out to be," he told himself dismally.

A scream sounded above, then shouts, and curses, and the rumble of soldiers' feet. A man's voice came echoing down into the dungeon. "Guards, everyone! Above! Above!"

The young soldier who had been sitting outside Noph's cell was suddenly gone, his chair no longer leaning against the wall but rattling dully where he had been.

There was a new catastrophe in the sanctuary above.

Noph's own voice echoed in his head: *Some hero you'll turn out to be if you give up now. They need you up there.*

From all of Waterdeep, the Open Lord had selected Noph to trust—Noph and three others. Just because Noph was accused of betraying that trust did not mean he was guilty of doing so.

Not yet, at least.

He stood up. In the dim light sifting into his cell, he began to study the walls and door for some means of escape. He'd get out of this cell, aid Piergeiron in the new conflict, and find the woman with the burr in her voice—no, not just her, but her whole clan of assassins.

A hero could do no less.

* * * * *

As the shadows fell about him, Piergeiron wearily
drew his sword. He glimpsed Eiolola's white face, eyes
wide, one hand clutching the gem at her throat.

Next moment, the warriors solidified, flame to flesh,
and dropped to the floor. With their descent, a magical
darkness also fell.

"Stay behind me," Piergeiron shouted to his bride. "I
don't want to kill you in this blackness."

Others were shouting or screaming. The rumble of
their voices was augmented by the shuffle of feet and the
thud of stumbling bodies. Overloaded benches groaned
and began to topple. Bolts squealed as their threads were
shredded loose. One bench went over, and then another,
and two more. Blinded guests foundered atop each other.

Those trapped beneath fallen comrades and overturned
benches soon seemed the lucky ones. Screams rang out as
the shadow warriors advanced into the crowd. The un-
armed and night-blind guests were no match for them.
Many Waterdhavians fell to swords and flails; more still
were simply shoved out of the way as the invaders came
on through the stygian hall.

They're after us, Piergeiron realized grimly. Only now
did his dread find its true cause. He thought, one of us will
not survive this.

The din of blind battle increased. The cries neared,
converging on the couple.

A shoulder knocked against Piergeiron's waist. Someone blundered into his legs. Panting, he raised his sword
overhead. In this black crush of panicked guests, he could

accidentally slay his own people. An elbow caught his jaw. Another body rammed into him. In moments, he was up to his shoulders in struggling, fleeing folk. At the edge of vision, he saw Kern attempting vainly to stem the tide. The flood of bodies pressed hard against Piergeiron, and he staggered. It was battle enough to keep to his feet in the mad press. He reeled.

"Eidola!" he shouted. "Are you still there?"

He could not hear her answer over the commotion, but felt her pressed, back to back, against him.

A man who had been rammed up beside Piergeiron suddenly was gone, sprawling onto the floor. Then another fell away, and another, until Eidola alone remained with him. The roar of panic was still around them, but the people had cleared away.

"It's just us now, Eidola. They want one or both of us." His blade sliced the air before them. "I wonder where Khelben has gotten off to."

Doggedly swinging Halcyon through a defensive drill, the Open Lord cried breathlessly to the attackers, "Who are you, and what business have you here?"

"You know our business, I'm sure, Lord Piergeiron," came a nasty voice. The dialect was like that of the western Heartlands, but with a nasal edge. "As to who we are, you must find that out yourselves."

"You have us at a disadvantage. You know us, but we do not know you. You clearly can see in this unnatural night, but we cannot," Piergeiron said, angered by the pleading tone in his own voice. He added in challenge, "Unless you are cowards, you would not fight this way."

"Would you battle me, Piergeiron Paladinson, even in

this darkness?"

"If the way is clear of my countrymen, I would fight and slay you, yes," growled Piergeiron.

"The way is clear, Open Lord," came the reply. "My warriors and I have cleared it. I challenge you to an honorable duel. My first officer will meanwhile fight your bride."

"I accept," said Piergeiron.

He closed his eyes—they were no good to him in this darkness anyway—and let his pure soul sense the presence of evil before him. Any true paladin, with concentration, could sense evil. Given practice, an elder paladin could almost *see* evil with his heart. Piergeiron concentrated. A smallish image came to his mind's eye—the faintly shimmering form of a warrior. Farther back stood the warrior's comrades, holding back the crowd.

In a whisper, Piergeiron asked Eidola, "Do you see them? Do you sense them—with your soul? Close your eyes. You can feel where they are—"

She was still behind him, but only silence answered his question.

"You can do it, Eidola," the Open Lord insisted. "Summon the *good* in you."

"Are you ready to die, Paladinson?" interrupted the nasty voice.

Piergeiron drew a deep breath and said a silent prayer to Torm the True: *Guide my sword, and guard my bride.* Then he turned toward the shimmering form. "Your evil betrays you, shadow man."

Raising his sword overhead, Piergeiron advanced on the figure. Halcyon swept downward in a deadly arc, and the shadow warrior jumped back.

"Not so blind, after all, eh Thickskull?" taunted the voice.

"There is blindness, and there is blindness," replied Piergeiron, swinging the blade again. It rushed in and rang off of a metal breastplate. At last, something to fight against. He followed with a third stroke, and this time the image seemed to wince.

"First blood to me," Piergeiron noted calmly.

"Last blood to me," responded the voice.

Piergeiron was surprised by a stinging blow to his side. He drew back, considering. This man was evil, but his sword was not; of course it did not appear in his mind's eye. That mistake would not be made twice.

Piergeiron darted in, quick for a man his size. He hurled a heavy blow down on his opponent. Sword rang on sword, then grated away to one side. Piergeiron followed the weight of his blade, turning its tip to drive inward. The shadow warrior was too fast, though, batting Halcyon away and sending out his own blow.

The Open Lord ducked back, then lunged, landing a second attack.

"I thought I would regret having to kill you," the warrior hissed in pain. "But I will not regret it at all."

* * * * *

The cell door proved rotten around its barred window. A repeated series of kicks to the bars at last tore them free of the spongy wood. The iron dropped to the ground and rattled loudly.

Now, Noph needed merely to wriggle through. . . . After a lot of shimmying, a few select curses, and one moment of panic when he was stuck halfway in and halfway out, Noph won free of the door and rolled out onto his shoulders. He let out a blast of air as he landed.

"Better my shoulders than my head," he muttered.

The reborn hero stood and brushed himself off. He took a deep breath. "Time for some true valor."

With that thought, Noph strode to the dim, winding stairs and climbed upward, toward the screaming above.

This dungeon is deep, he thought, breathless. The steps seem to wind forever. It didn't take half as long to be dragged down here . . . of course, other legs did that work.

After his fourth circuit of the stairs, Noph saw a light above. The roar of battle had redoubled. By his sixth circuit, he reached a round doorway. Noph darted through it into a hallway. He halted, panting.

Which way to the sanctuary?

After a moment of indecision, he followed the echoing cries down the hall. In no time, he had reached the narthex.

Ahead of him, a shimmering curtain of darkness stretched across the doorway. A few nobles staggered out, their hands groping blindly forward. When they entered the light, the folk blinked in astonishment before gathering their wits and darting away from the sanctuary as quickly as they could.

Bring them out. That's what a hero would do here. Lead the people from the darkness into the light.

One more deep breath, and into the crowded chaos he plunged.

* * * * *

Khelben writhed beneath an agonizing weight. It had fallen upon him just when the shadow warriors appeared. It had fallen with the very weight of the palace itself.

He had seen only the flare of candles, figures taking shape out of flames. Then, as the warriors became flesh and leapt to the floor, the terrific crushing blackness had fallen atop the Lord Mage of Waterdeep.

He gasped, air seeping damnably slowly into and out of his lungs. He struggled to hold to consciousness, all his spells lost beneath numb fingers.

Whatever magic had brought these warriors here, it was ancient—a sorcery that could shatter worlds.

* * * * *

Noph had made numerous forays into the wheeling black chaos of the sanctuary. Because of his efforts, hundreds of guests had fled to safety. Their battered rescuer did not even waste time watching them flee but rushed back for more souls.

It was dangerous work in that unnatural darkness. Each time Noph grappled a given guest, he was paid back with a royal pummeling. In a battle at midnight, saviors and slayers are hard to distinguish. In payment for his assistance, Noph had received two black eyes and a broken nose, as well as bruises and scratches all over his body.

Once he had wrestled a guest into the light, though, it was a different story. Some were almost penitent. A few even apologized, or kissed him on the very cheek they had previously punched. All of them, though, quickly turned about and pelted for the nearest exit.

Noph returned to the sanctuary. Plunging back into the darkness felt much like diving into a cold sea where sailors drowned amid frenzied sharks.

This time, though, when his hand caught hold of a woman's arm, she shouted out with an unmistakable Calashite burr, "Let go of me!"

"Ah," he replied. "Music to my ears."

With newfound energy, Noph wrestled the woman into a headlock—he imagined her still with a lizard head—and hauled her kicking and screaming into the light.

Instead of letting her go, he dragged her onward, and down the steps of a very deep dungeon.

* * * * *

Unsure where the warrior's blade would strike next, Piergeiron countered with a wide sweep of his own. Steel edges rang against each other. Piergeiron twisted Halcyon, entangling the man's weapon. He struggled to fling the sword to ground, but the shadow figure held the pommel tight. Blades slid and scraped, pushing off to one side.

Piergeiron stepped up next to the warrior and stomped on his foot. The shock and pain jarred the man's hand loose. Piergeiron twisted his foe's sword free and flung it to the ground. Then he kicked the warrior's good leg out from under him and swung Halcyon to bear on the man's throat.

"Surrender, all of you, and I will spare this one," Piergeiron commanded.

Laughter came from the circle of warriors around. "Go ahead and kill him. It's your right, and we never liked him anyway."

"I will fight every last one of you," Piergeiron warned. "I will *slay* every last one of you."

More laughter. "Open Lord, if your soul can see so well, why don't you take a look around?"

He did, sensing the ring of warriors, twenty strong, on all sides of him. "So you have us surrounded. If you were men of honor, you would come one at a time to fight me."

"Maybe you can see us with those paladin eyes of yours," jeered one of the warriors. "Maybe you can sense the presence of evil all around you, but what about the presence of good? What about your bride? Where might she be?"

Piergeiron whirled, his hand out. "Eidola? Where are you?"

There came no response except the guffaws of the warriors.

"Where is she? What have you done?"

The shadow warriors were withdrawing, their circle widening around Piergeiron. The Open Lord charged the nearest one, skewering him with his sword. As the man fell dead beneath him, Piergeiron pulled Halcyon free and rushed onward. He stumbled over a fallen bench and the bodies beneath it.

The warriors continued to retreat, picking their way through the wreckage of the sanctuary. Piergeiron thrashed forward a few steps more, but was dragged down again by smashed wood and groaning forms.

The invaders had reached the far walls of the chamber.

Each turned and stood, stationed before the ensconced candles. Their bodies suddenly leapt up, forming six-foot high flames.

Piergeiron shielded his eyes from the sudden light, as did the remaining stragglers and dying victims in the ruined chapel. Then, with a pop, the candle flames shrank inward and disappeared. Darkness again settled over the smoldering ruins of midnight.

Chapter 7
For Worse

"Anything yet?" asked Piergeiron. He leaned against a wall of Khelben's laboratories and watched the slow dripping of the mage's Kara-Turian water clock. Aside from requesting updates, Piergeiron could well have been a statue.

"I said five more minutes," Khelben noted testily. The Lord Mage was stooped over a pile of books that were sprawled open atop each other.

"It has been four minutes thirty-eight seconds," the Open Lord noted dully.

"I said five minutes," Khelben repeated.

Piergeiron said no more, still pressed against the cold stone wall.

In the remaining twenty-two seconds, Khelben flipped the pages of several tomes, consulting charts and tables. When ten seconds were left, he looked up irately at his friend. With an off-handed flick of his wrist, Khelben cast a slow spell upon the water clock. Its constant gurgling slowed until it was nearly stopped. There was no reason to slow Piergeiron as well. The man could not be slower and still live.

Khelben sighed, and worked another two hours. When he was done, he dispelled his enchantment.

Piergeiron blinked. "Ah, five minutes."

"Here it is," replied Khelben. "I've been searching ancient texts for references to spells or artifacts characterized by their dweomer draw. What crushed me to the ground was a sorcery of great magnitude."

"And?" Piergeiron asked listlessly.

"I found three possible artifacts, two of which were unlikely due to the—"

"And, which one?" Piergeiron asked.

"A Bloodforge. It was a Bloodforge that created that army."

"What is a—"

"It's an artifact of great antiquity, a device that can form armies out of thin air."

"Each candle was a Bloodforge?" asked Piergeiron.

The mage shook his head in consideration. "No, but

each was linked to a Bloodforge somehow. They allowed the forged warriors to gate into the palace and back out again." He cleared his throat. "As far as I know, the only place where Bloodforges are found is the Utter East."

"The Utter East?"

The mage nodded. "The candles confirm it. They were an engagement present sent to Eidola from an unknown benefactor, who suggested their use in the wedding. Though the giver is unknown, the crate in which the candles came is stamped with border seals that stretch from Waterdeep all the way down to the Utter East."

"Even if I have to travel the whole world, I will find her," said Piergeiron wearily.

"And what of Waterdeep when you are gone? What of the trade route and all the other programs you have worked so hard to implement?" Khelben pointed out. "Running out across half the world is a job for the young, Piergeiron. For those with nothing better to do. Send someone else."

"How could I?" the Open Lord muttered. "How could I trust Eidola to anyone else?"

"Are you so arrogant as to think you are the greatest warrior in Faerûn?"

Piergeiron looked chagrined.

Khelben went on, "And isn't trust something that has set you in good stead until now?"

Piergeiron dropped his head toward his chest and slowly nodded.

* * * * *

The Blackstaff stood at the door to Piergeiron's drawing room. His knuckles rapped lightly on the frame. "Open Lord, I have brought him, as you requested."

From the plush darkness of woolen carpets and velvet drapes came a faint summons. "Come in."

The wizard silently drew back the door and, with a smooth wave of a hand, gestured the lad forward.

Noph had looked better, certainly. Both his eyes were black, his nose had been set with sticks and torn cloth, and his lip was split in two places. He favored one leg as he came in, a crutch jammed under his arm. Though Noph had publicly abnegated his nobility and subsequently been disowned by his father, he still carried himself with the bearing of a nobleman as he bowed deeply before the Open Lord.

No, not the bearing of a nobleman, but that of a hero.

Piergeiron's own wounds were in interior spaces. Though the body that slumped in the chair before Noph was the same well-dressed and athletic figure as before, Piergeiron's eyes were as dark and empty as the burned-out Eye of Ao.

"Ahem," Khelben said, standing there beside the lad. "Open Lord, remember, you wanted to see him?"

"Yes," replied Piergeiron. He offered no more comment.

Khelben's black brows drew down, and he prompted, "Something about rewarding his heroism. . . . Beyond releasing him from the dungeon. . . ."

"Yes."

The master mage turned toward the tattered lad. "The Open Lord is in need of your service, Kastonoph. He needs men he can trust, especially now."

Noph nodded humbly. "I could use the work—"

"It's more than just trustworthiness. If it weren't for you, the crossbow would have gone off as those rogue mariners had planned, and we would have had no idea who had done it."

"I can start right away—" Noph said.

"You single-handedly foiled a guild plot against Lady Eidola. You caught the ringleader, squeezed a confession from her, and rounded up the others—not to mention the scrap of cloth that was the chief evidence against the second-in-command. If it wasn't for you, we would have thought the assassins from the mariners guild were in league with the dopplegangers or the agents from the Utter East. You and you alone solved the one mystery that has been solved here—"

Noph wore a wondering look as he studied the Lord Mage's face. "If your concern is money, I wouldn't need more than bed and board—"

"Damn it, son—you're making this only more difficult," snapped Khelben. His eyebrows thickened like twin storm clouds. "I am not accustomed to being a messenger boy for the Open Lord, or anyone—"

"What the Blackstaff is trying and failing to say," interrupted Piergeiron quietly, "is that I owe you a deep apology. I placed my trust in you once, and it was well placed. I should not have doubted you."

Noph colored, unsure how to respond to the apology of the Open Lord of Waterdeep. He waved a dismissive hand. "Bygones."

"And not only do I and all Waterdeep owe you a debt of gratitude, but we have further need of your heroism. We yet do not know what the dopplegangers had plotted, or for whom they worked. And we have no idea yet who those shadow warriors were, where exactly they came from, and where they took Eido—" The Open Lord's voice, until then a thready whisper, was choked away into silence.

"He wants you to aid a group of paladins we are gathering to rescue his bride," Khelben supplied. "Would you be interested in such an appointment?"

Something of Noph's former spirit returned. "I go to watch."

Postlude

Wrong Side of the Mirror

Oh, to sleep. . . .
It is all I want to do.
This weariness is the sort that denies sleep.
Perhaps if I slept, I could keep the dust of my pulverized world from filtering down through my eyes and mind and into my very soul. Perhaps if I slept, I would be letting go like the very dust itself. After all, what once bound all to all is gone now. Everything solid melts into air.

Shaleen, it is as if you died again.

What has happened to me, to the Open Lord of Waterdeep?

What once bound all to all?

Oh, to sleep. . . .

WELCOME TO THE UTTER EAST!

THE DOUBLE DIAMOND TRIANGLE SAGA

The story continues . . .

The bride of the Open Lord of Waterdeep has been abducted. The kidnappers are from the far-off lands of the Utter East. But who are they? And what do they really want? Now a group of brave paladins must travel to the perilous kingdoms of this unknown land to find the answers. But in this mysterious world, nothing is ever quite what it appears.

Look for the forthcoming books in the series

The Paladins
(January 1998)

The Mercenaries
(January 1998)

Errand of Mercy
(February 1998)

An Opportunity for Profit
(March 1998)

Conspiracy
(April 1998)

Uneasy Alliances
(May 1998)

Easy Betrayals
(June 1998)

The Diamond
(July 1998)

Coming in January

THE PALADINS
By James M. Ward and David Wise

The fantasy serial novel that began with *The Abduction* continues. The bride of the Lord of Waterdeep has been kidnapped. Now the lord himself has fallen ill. His loyal followers prepare to rescue the abducted woman, little knowing what perils their quest will bring them up against in the far-off realm of the Utter East. Prepare for adventure in the company of the paladins.

THE MERCENARIES
By Ed Greenwood

In the mysterious land of the Utter East, a shadowy figure hires a group of unemployed pirates to aid him in a dangerous mission. What is their connection to the kidnapping of a young bride that has taken place in the faraway city of Waterdeep? Behind the mission lies a hidden purpose. Yet secrets may be revealed as you follow the quest of the mercenaries.

Coming in February

ERRAND OF MERCY
By Roger E. Moore

The paladins sent by the Lord of Waterdeep to rescue his kidnapped bride have arrived in a kingdom of the Utter East. The monarch seems friendly; but the kingdom is beset by menacing fiends. Before the ruler agrees to help the paladins in their quest, there is just one small task they must perform . . . .